W9-AUD-655

Dinosaur School

DINOSAURS AT SCHOOL

Please visit our website, www.garethstevens.com. For a free color catalog of all our high-quality books, call toll free 1-800-542-2595 or fax 1-877-542-2596.

Library of Congress Cataloging-in-Publication Data

Appleby, Alex.
Dinosaurs at school / by Alex Appleby.
    p. cm. — (Dinosaur school)
ISBN 978-1-4339-9042-7 (pbk.)
ISBN 978-1-4339-9043-4 (6-pack)
ISBN 978-1-4339-9041-0 (library binding)
1. Schools—Juvenile literature. 2. School day—Juvenile literature. I. Appleby, Alex. II. Title.
LB1513.A66 2014
371.8'72—dc23

First Edition

Published in 2014 by
Gareth Stevens Publishing
111 East 14th Street, Suite 349
New York, NY 10003

Designer: Andrea Davison-Bartolotta
Editor: Ryan Nagelhout

All illustrations by Planman Technologies

Printed in the United States of America

CPSIA compliance information: Batch #CS13GS: For further information contact Gareth Stevens, New York, New York at 1-800-542-2595.

DINOSAURS AT SCHOOL

By Alex Appleby

Gareth Stevens
Publishing

I see my school.

I see a flag.

I see a school bus.

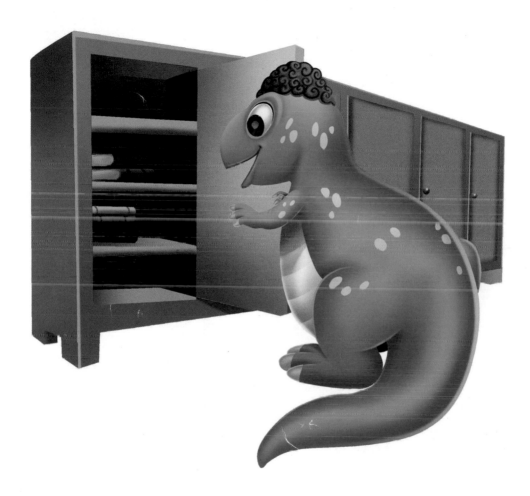

I see a locker.

7

I see a pencil.

I see a pen.

I see a crayon.

I see a paintbrush.

I see a bookcase.

I see a book.

I see a teacher.

I see a backpack.

I see a computer.

I see a ruler.

I see letters.

I see numbers.

I see a ball.

I see my friend.

I see a desk.

I see a chair.

Dinosaurs at School

ball

crayon

paintbrush

book

desk

pen

bookcase

letters

pencil

chair

numbers

ruler

24